HER CHRISTMAS CRUSH

A CAPROCK CANYON PREQUEL

BREE LIVINGSTON

Edited by
CHRISTINA SCHRUNK

Bree Livingston Publishing LLC

Her Christmas Crush

Copyright © 2021 by **Bree Livingston**

Edited by Christina Schrunk

https://www.facebook.com/christinaschrunk.editor

Proofread by Krista R. Burdine

https://www.facebook.com/iamgrammaresque

Bree Livingston

https://www.breelivingston.com

Her Christmas Crush/ Bree Livingston. -- 1st ed.

ISBN: 9798736063291

CHAPTER 1

*R*ushing out of the house, Caroline Nell grabbed her purse. If she was late for the Christmas Festival committee one more time, she'd be ousted for sure. Even if she was one of the only people who'd volunteered to help this year.

Was it really her fault that her teacher conferences at the elementary school ran late? She couldn't just shove a parent out the school door with a, *Sorry, that Christmas Festival isn't going to plan itself.*

As she got to her car, her phone rang, and she put it on speaker. She'd had it handy, knowing Pauline would call. "I'm on my way."

"Where are you?" her best friend asked.

"I had to stop by the house and change."

The bark of a giggle filled her car. "Ohhh...change.

Right."

Rolling her eyes, Caroline sighed. "It's not because of him." Just because a rumor was going around that their festival director had asked him to help out didn't mean the man would actually volunteer. He worked at the ranch twenty minutes away, and he probably had better things to do in his off time. "One of my students tripped and spilled chocolate milk all down my shirt. I had to clean up a little."

"Sure you did," Pauline teased. "It couldn't possibly be that King West might be at the meeting tonight."

King Taylor West. Oh, how she'd crushed on him in high school. Not that she ever thought she had a shot, but he'd recently returned to Caprock Canyon after attending school in Houston for agriculture. He'd been dreamy in high school, but now in his mid-twenties? Holy wow, he was gorgeous.

The man had a head of thick hair begging to be finger-combed, dark blue eyes like a Texas Sky, broad shoulders, rough hands, and a smile to end all smiles. As captain of the chess club, Caroline wasn't exactly in his league, but it didn't stop her from dreaming.

"Earth to Caroline." Pauline laughed.

"Oh, shush," she said, cranking the engine. Instead of a smooth roar to life, there was nothing. Trying again, she whispered, "Come on, start."

"What?" Pauline asked.

"My car won't start." Caroline touched her forehead to the steering wheel. It was Friday, and the shop would be closed for the weekend. "Guess I'm walking for the next few days."

The faint sound of the meeting being called to order filtered from the phone. "I gotta go, Caroline. I'll let the director know about your car."

Fantastic. She'd been late to almost every meeting, and she'd sworn on her Grandma Jo's cookies she'd be on time for their next one. Picking up the plate of baked goodies her grandma had given her, she pushed out of the car. "Thanks. I'll be there as quick as I can."

The line went dead, and she dropped the phone into the abyss that was her purse. She could call someone for a lift, but most, if not all, of her family and friends were already at the meeting. That was life in a small town.

Hugging the container of cookies to her chest, she began walking the four blocks to the high school gymnasium. As she walked, she hummed "Silent Night," one of the songs they were using for the festival.

Clouds moved in from the northwest, and a lazy cool breeze hit her skin through the oversized sweater she wore. Why had on earth had she picked a sweater to wear? In the same breath, she answered, "Because you weren't walking when you picked it out."

That would fix her. The next time—and she knew there would be a next time—she'd just pick a coat. Although, that's what she told herself the last time her car wouldn't start, and here she was, two-shoeing it to the gym again in a flimsy sweater. She really needed to get her car to the shop so she could figure out why the battery was fine one minute and not the next.

A light-orange seventies pickup passed her, stopped, and then backed up. Another benefit of living in a small town. If someone saw you walking, more often than not, they'd give you a ride, especially if they were a local.

Caroline stopped at the driver's window and gulped. King West? She was sure he had a new pickup. "Hello, King. What happened to the blue one?"

His eyebrows knitted together. "What?"

"That nice big blue pickup you were driving. Is it in the shop already?" she asked.

Chuckling, he shook his head. "Aw, I don't need new. I sold it. This old one here is good enough."

That wasn't really an answer, but it was his business. "Oh, okay." She started walking again.

"Caroline, wait," King called, leaning out of his

pickup. "Are you meeting with the festival committee?"

She turned, her pulse jumping at the sound of her name spoken in his deep baritone voice. "Uh, yeah. Why?"

"That's where I'm going. Wanna ride?"

Her mouth went dry. A ride? With King? In a single-cab pickup?

His eyebrows lifted to his hairline. "Uh, hello?"

Say something, girl. Just when she thought she'd never get her tongue unglued from the roof of her mouth, she nodded. "Yeah, that'd be great."

He gave her another one of his heartbreaker smiles. "Come on, then. Any later, and Mrs. Tam won't be happy with either of us."

Without another word, she hurried to the passenger door, but before she could get there, he'd already opened it from inside. Shutting the door, she said, "Thank you. I can give you some gas money or something for giving me a lift."

"We're going the same way. Not that big of a deal." He shot her a half-smile. "What's in the container?"

"Container?" She blinked.

"Yeah, the one you're holding on to like someone might try to steal it." He laughed. It was a terrific laugh. Deep and warm and knee-weakening.

Shaking her head, she said, "Oh, uh, these are cookies my grandma made. They're to appease Mrs. Tam."

"Then I'm definitely glad I picked you up. Maybe they'll distract her from both of us being late." He winked.

Seriously, he needed to stop. Her brain and mouth were already having connection issues. "I'm sure they will. She loves my grandma's cookies." Caroline chewed her lip. "Uh, I didn't realize you were on the committee. When did you volunteer?"

"Oh, Mrs. Tam caught me earlier this week and asked me."

"Yeah, we needed a little more muscle. Mrs. Tam will appreciate your joining."

"Even more so when I show up with someone holding cookies." He grinned. "Are they chocolate chip?"

Caroline shook her head. "No, they're peanut butter."

His lips turned down. "Not my favorite."

"And chocolate chip is?"

"One of them. I like oatmeal too. My favorite is chocolate chewy ones." He shrugged. "But a cookie is a cookie, and a smart man never turns down homemade goodies."

The gym came into view, and Caroline tried to hide her disappointment. She'd had the chance to ride in the same vehicle as King West, and it was coming to an end.

Parking the truck, he said, "Don't move."

"Okay." She blinked. Maybe there was a trick with the door or something she wasn't aware of.

King jogged around the front of the pickup and opened her door. "A gentleman always opens the door for a lady."

If he kept this up, she'd need to carry a water bottle. At the rate she was going, she'd need a river to keep her mouth from going dry. "You didn't when you picked me up."

"We were already late, though I did open it from the inside," he said, flashing another killer smile her way. "I hoped you'd forgive me for that one time."

"I forgive you." She swallowed hard and whispered, "Guess we better get in there."

Without waiting for him, she nearly broke her neck trying to get inside. If she didn't know better, he was flirting with her. That was impossible, though. There was no way that man was interested in her. The very thought was ridiculous to even consider. What she needed was to just concentrate on the meeting and forget silly notions.

CHAPTER 2

*D*id he smell? King West discreetly checked himself. Nope, he'd put deodorant on. So why did Caroline Nell run away so fast? He realized he wasn't the smoothest guy on the planet, but he was pretty sure his overt flirting sent signals the space station could see.

He'd only been back in Caprock Canyon a couple of months, but he'd been kept busy on the ranch. Since returning, he'd had his eye on the cute elementary teacher. At first, he thought someone new had moved to town. Finding out it was the chess club captain and that they'd graduated the same year had thrown him. He couldn't remember her being so beautiful.

With her cute little sweater and jeans, he'd almost swallowed his tongue as he'd driven by her on the way to the meeting. She had curves in all the right places, long dark hair, and blue eyes as dark as his. Plus, those Cupid's-bow pink lips. They'd been right there, and they were the most kissable pair of lips he'd ever seen on a woman.

Setting his hands on his hips, he shook his head as he followed at a less breakneck speed into the gym. It had been a while since he'd been inside. Champion banners from his time on the basketball team still adorned the walls.

"Mr. West, thank you for coming." Mrs. Tam's voice boomed from the front of the building where about a dozen people were gathered around a table. Growing up in a small town, he knew most of them.

"Sorry I'm late. A calf was caught in wire, and I had to run home and wash up," he said as he took a seat next to the retired teacher.

Lifting an eyebrow, she said, "Acceptable excuse," then eyed Caroline. "Unlike others."

As soon as the woman's gaze drifted away, he leaned forward, catching Caroline rolling her eyes and mouthing something he couldn't figure out. It was cute. Well, all of her was cute. He'd hoped joining the committee would give him a chance to ask her out.

"Before we get started this evening, I'd like to ask for two volunteers to be in charge. With my mother being bedbound with her hip, I'll not be able to contribute as much of my time as I normally do in the final couple of weeks. So, anyone?"

From what he understood, the festival this year was working to raise money for new playground equipment for the elementary school. When Mrs. Tam called him, asking if he'd like to join to help their cause, she listed off a few names of the members, and Caroline had been one of them. That was all the motivation he'd needed.

People murmured amongst themselves with no one really jumping at the chance. Mrs. Tam had run the committee for two nearly flawless decades. Anyone who did it would be judged by her past performances. Which was most likely the reason behind asking for two volunteers. It would take that many to fill the woman's shoes.

Finally, King raised his hand. The elementary school needed that playground equipment. His hope was that his children would use it someday. "I'll do it."

Not a second passed before someone said, "Caroline Nell said she'd love to lead."

As King leaned forward again, Caroline came into view, looking like a deer in the headlights. He got the distinct impression she hadn't volunteered on her own.

"Can you manage to arrive on time?" Mrs. Tam asked, slightly lifting her nose in the air and looking down at Caroline.

Her lips pinched together ever so slightly as she glared at a familiar-looking woman sitting next to her. "Yes, I can. There are no more parent-teacher conferences this year, and I plan to get my car fixed."

Mrs. Tam smiled. "Wonderful."

"Did you already have a theme in mind?" Caroline asked.

Shaking her head, the director said, "No, I've been a little too distracted since my mother fell. I thought we could discuss it since this is the first meeting."

"Oh, okay." Caroline's eyes locked with King's, and she squeaked, a blanket of pink covering her cheeks.

This was as perfect as King could have hoped. He'd agreed to help because it looked like no one else would, but his mom had always said giving back was the best reward. She wasn't wrong. He smiled at Caroline and winked.

The blush on her cheeks darkened. After that, she didn't look his direction. All through the meeting, he caught himself casting glances in her direction in the hopes of catching her gaze again.

Once they were done discussing all the particulars, Mrs. Tam adjourned the meeting. He waited as the small group cleared out before approaching Caroline, who was talking with the familiar-looking woman who had volunteered Caroline.

"I'm sorry to interrupt," he said, slipping his hands into his pockets. "I was hoping Caroline and I could talk about festival plans."

The woman Caroline was speaking to stuck out her hand. "I'm Pauline. I was in the chess club with Caroline when we were in high school."

King nodded, pulling his hand out to shake hers. "Oh, that's right. I knew you looked familiar. How have you been?"

"Fine." She smiled and looked at Caroline. "Well, I'd love to stay and catch up, but I've got to get home. I forgot…something." She hurried off, laughing.

Caroline smiled. "Uh, hi, again."

"Looks like we're decorating a gym for the Christmas festival."

"Looks so. I guess we should maybe figure out times to meet to discuss what we'd like to do."

King pulled his phone out to check the time. "The diner is still open. We've got about an hour or so."

"Okay." She smiled, bringing attention to her lips. If they weren't as soft as they looked, he'd eat his hat. "That should be plenty of time."

In his mind, not hardly. He had a feeling there

wasn't enough time when it came to her. "I'll drop you home after. Sound okay?"

"Sure."

As their gazes locked, his pulse raced faster. Now he wished he'd paid more attention to her in high school. Oh, yeah, there was something special about her. With a little luck, he'd find out just how special she was.

CHAPTER 3

*I*f Caroline continued to pinch herself, her entire thigh would be one big blue bruise, but she couldn't stop herself. Surely, she had to be dreaming that she was once again in King West's truck...driving to a diner...to have dinner with him.

Sure, it was only to discuss the festival. That didn't stop her from dreaming up all sorts of situations that led to him kissing her. Why was she even thinking things like that? This was their first time ever really talking to each other. Even for her, that was moving a little fast.

He was super cute in high school, and he was heart-racing attractive now. But looks weren't something you built a future on. What if all he had was on the outside? She wanted more than good looks. When she dreamed of a husband, he was romantic and sweet. She hadn't run in the same circles with King in high school and didn't really know him.

"You're awful quiet over there. Something on your mind?" he asked, stopping at one of the two stoplights in town.

Right, like she'd share that. Not a chance. "Nothing really. Do you have any ideas about a theme?" A few had been discussed in the meeting, but nothing was concrete.

He leaned forward and looked up at the sky. "As wet as it's been this year, we may have snow. We could do white wonderland."

It had been rainy, and this was one of only a few days in the weekly forecast that was dry. That did give a little hope that it would be white for Christmas. "That's not too bad of an idea."

"You say that like you're surprised." He laughed. "I'm trying to decide if I should be offended."

"You *are* a jock." She grinned.

He grasped his chest. "You wound me, woman. You wound me."

She batted at his arm. "Stop, goofball. That's not how I meant it." Twisting in the seat, she faced him. "Now, what did you have in mind?"

"I don't know. If it does happen to snow, maybe we

could have a snowman-building contest, do a hot chocolate competition, and the children's choir could perform in the gazebo across from the high school. We could cover it in little white lights and pine garland. Maybe we could even do a sleigh ride."

It didn't sound too bad, but they'd always kept the festival rather simple with treats and hot cider to drink. The businesses in town would donate prizes to auction off. This year, the money would go toward replacing the playground equipment. It was older than Moses and only a strip of duct tape away from falling apart.

"We've never done anything like that before."

He glanced at her. "Doesn't mean we can't start something."

For a split second, it almost seemed like he was talking about something other than the festival. That couldn't be right. She was just frazzled because he was a good-looking man that she'd crushed on since she could remember. Shaking her head, she replied, "No, it doesn't. It's a little ambitious for two weeks, don't you think?"

"Well, I know the Klines would be more than willing to let us use a couple of their horses." The light turned green, and he took a left. "If we do happen to have a white Christmas, I have a friend who has access to a sleigh."

"A sleigh. I think that would be nice." It didn't take much for her to picture being snuggled against King. "I know I'd like that."

King nodded. "Okay, so the sleigh is a definite, then. Do you have any ideas?"

Shrugging, she bounced her knee. "I like the snow-man-building idea, and even the hot chocolate competition. That actually sounds really fun. I think the children's choir should perform first. That way they aren't too strung out on sugar."

As King parked the pickup, he turned to her. "Sounds like words of wisdom to me."

"Thanks." She grinned as her cheeks burned again. What was it about this man that made her so mushy?

"Let's talk more inside," he said, getting out of the pickup and walking to her side. After opening her door, he stopped her from getting out. "There's a puddle I didn't see when I parked. Let me help you out."

His hands gripped her around the waist, and in an instant, she was sure she fully understood what getting hit by lightning would feel like. There wasn't a nerve in her body that wasn't on fire.

Setting her feet on the ground, he smiled. "There. Now you won't get your feet wet."

The bones in her neck were just as affected as her nerves as she bobbed her head up and down. "Uh-huh."

Reaching behind her, he shut the passenger door. "You all right?"

"Uh-huh." She blinked and shook her head. "I'm good. Hungry. Starved even."

Grinning, he said, "Good thing we're here, then."

"Guess so."

King would have to stop touching her if she was going to be functional. She needed to keep her feet on the ground. Maybe he was a great guy. Wonderful even. It also seemed as though he was flirting with her.

Sheesh, he was really messing with her head. How was she going to plan a festival if she didn't stop turning to mush when he looked at her? She was a teacher, for goodness sakes. Every day, she managed to wrangle her eight-year-old students. She should be able to get herself in line with no problem.

Pulling her shoulders back, she decided she'd handle this whole thing like a professional. There'd be no more nonsense.

Fat chance, her heart said and snorted. This man spelled trouble with a capital H...Heartbreak Hotel.

CHAPTER 4

*K*ing kept his attention on his menu spread out in front of him on the table, but he could feel Caroline's gaze on him every few seconds as she peeked over the one in her hand. It was adorable. *She* was adorable. He liked her quick wit and her smile.

There was no denying she was a catch and a half, and he'd only spent a little time with her. No doubt he'd find that to be fact once he got to know her. The draw to her seemed to only grow stronger the longer he was around her.

Again, she hid her face behind the menu, and he couldn't stop himself. "Why are you peeking at me?"

Caroline jumped enough that the booth she was in rattled a little, and she hid her face again. "I wasn't."

He lifted his gaze and smiled. "You're holding that menu upside down."

"Uh…" She quickly set the menu down. "Because I knew what I wanted."

"Really?" he said, tilting his head. "What caught your eye? Maybe I'd enjoy it too."

Her eyes widened, and it took everything in him to not laugh. If she continued to be this cute, he'd have no choice but to kiss her when he dropped her off.

"Pancakes with blueberries. And coffee to drink."

"That sounds pretty good. I think I'll have the same." He'd never had that particular item before, but he was interested to hear what her reply would be.

She caught her bottom lip with her teeth. "With bacon."

Bacon. Now that was a love language. "Sounds even better."

Narrowing her eyes, she smiled and said, "And Tabasco sauce."

He wasn't much for hot sauce, but he could hold his own if challenged. "I like it hot."

Her smile vanished in a blink. "You like hot sauce?"

"I'm a Texan. I think it's required by law."

A tiny giggle bubbled from her. "I think you might be right." She lifted an eyebrow. "I guess we have something in common."

"I guess we do." And it only took a little to get the conversation moving. "How long have you been back in Caprock Canyon?"

"About two years ago. I thought my grandma Jo needed someone close in case something happened." She shrugged. "Plus, I love living here."

Nodding, he said, "I do too. There's something about small town life, isn't there?"

Before Caroline could answer, the waitress stopped at the table. "King West. Well, I'll be. I haven't seen you in a long time." Smiling, she put her back to Caroline. "When did you get back in town?"

King remembered her. Ruthie Dun was the most popular girl in school, and she'd set her sights on King for a while during his senior year. He'd quickly learned that she ran at a speed that was entirely too fast for him. "Hi, Ruthie. I got back a few months ago. Did I hear you married Zack Carter?"

Her smile faltered. "You heard right, but they shoulda mentioned we divorced two years ago. He simply had no ambition." She placed her hand on King's shoulder. "I'm only working here while I get my cosmetology license, and then I'm opening my own shop."

Ruthie went to run her fingers through his hair, and he ducked. "That's nice." He scooted closer to the wall.

"Caroline and I volunteered to help with the festival. We could use some coffee while we go over the details."

Looking down her nose, Ruthie turned to Caroline. "Oh, hi, Caroline. I didn't see you there." There was no missing the disdain in her voice. That didn't sit right with him.

"I'm sure you didn't." Caroline kept her gaze on her menu.

Ruthie smiled at King again. "I'll get that coffee right over."

The moment Ruthie was gone, King switched sides to sit next to Caroline. He hoped the message was loud and clear that he wasn't interested when the woman returned. There was nothing she had that he wanted.

Unlike the woman he was sitting next to now. Just being near her had every one of his nerves alert. "I'm glad you wanted coffee."

Caroline shrugged. "It's a little late, and I could have used decaf. Ruthie's always had a knack for making me feel invisible."

"Why? She's just jealous because you're so pretty."

Her head jerked up as her mouth parted, seeming surprised. "What?"

"Are you telling me you don't know you're gorgeous? 'Cause you are." He pushed back a stray lock that had fallen from her ponytail. "Prettiest girl I've ever seen."

"Oh."

Coffee mugs clacked against the table, and King looked up. Ruthie was giving him a death stare. If King was less of a gentleman, he'd laugh at her.

"Thank you for the coffee, Ruthie." Moving closer to Caroline, he put his arm around her shoulders. "We appreciate it."

A fake smile worthy of an Emmy spread on Ruthie's lips. "My pleasure. Have you decided what you'd like to order?"

"Yes, ma'am. We'd love blueberry pancakes with a side of bacon." He held her gaze a moment before returning his attention to Caroline. "Did you really want hot sauce?"

With a slight shake of her head, her lips quirked up. "No, I just wanted to see what you'd say."

He looked back up at Ruthie. "Seems that'll do us, Ruthie."

She pulled out her order pad and scribbled on it. "With bacon, right?"

"Yep. Thanks so much."

"I'll have it out as quick as I can." She sauntered off, throwing him a glare over her shoulder.

He turned to Caroline. "You think she got the message that I'm not interested?"

For a moment, she held his gaze and then nodded. "I think so."

"Good. Because I'm not."

"I don't come here very often." She chuckled. "Actually, I don't go anywhere very often. I mostly stay at home."

That surprised him. "Really?"

Shrugging, her gaze dipped to the table, her long lashes fanning against her cheeks.

Whatever her answer, King would consider himself lucky that she was still single, and he wouldn't take his fortune for granted either. His plans now included her, indefinitely or until she got sick of him.

Lifting her gaze to his, she said, "Yeah, really. Typically, I'm grading, but I wanted to help with the festival this year."

"Oh." It was all his brain could muster. She had him more tongue-tied than he'd ever been. He swallowed hard. "First year, huh?"

"Yeah, and based on Mrs. Tam, maybe my last if I don't start showing up on time."

He could help fix that. "Why don't I start picking you up for the meetings? We can talk festival and both be on time. That sound good to you?"

Heartbeat after heartbeat ticked by until he thought she might turn him down, an arrow that hit him dead center in the heart. Maybe she wasn't as interested as he hoped she might be.

He began to retract his offer. "I mean, if you'd like. I don't—"

"I'd love that," she said in a rush. "You know, being on time for the meetings."

"Good. I look—"

"Order's here," Ruthie chimed as she set their plates on the table. "I hope you like them, King."

Apparently, the girl was a little slower than he thought. "I'm sure we'll love them."

"Mine are cold," Caroline said.

King pressed his fingers against her stack of pancakes, and sure enough, they were shy a few degrees of downright frozen. "Yeah, her stack is cold."

Ruthie touched the locked attached to her necklace. "Are they? I'm so sorry. They're all we have, though."

His dander was rising. "I see. Well, why don't you bring a clean plate to the table, and I'll share mine with her."

"We're closing in just twenty minutes, and the dishwasher is already putting plates up." Ruthie held his gaze. "I might have something. I'll go check."

As she trotted off, King turned to Caroline. "I get the distinct impression she's being spiteful."

Caroline chuckled. "She's been that way a while. Zack fooled around on her, and I think the only way she knows how to deal with it is to share her misery."

King nodded as he looked in Ruthie's direction. "That may be, but that's no reason to treat you poorly."

"You don't have to share your pancakes with me. I'll be okay until I get home."

"You wanted blueberry pancakes, and you'll get them." He pushed her plate away and set his still-steaming stack between them. I do know how to share." He cut the stack down the middle. "There. How's that?"

A smile brightened her face. "It's great."

Oh, man, if he saw that sweet face every day for the rest of his life, it wouldn't be enough. And he'd been the source of her smile. By goodness, he liked her. A simple girl with simple tastes and cute to boot. Now all he needed to do was get to know her good and proper.

The idea tickled him all the way to his toes. Yep, Caprock Canyon just got a heap more exciting for him.

CHAPTER 5

"Thank you for bringing me home," Caroline said as King stopped at her front door. He hadn't just dumped her and run. He'd walked her to her front door, and that was after opening her door as he had every time they got in and out of his truck that night. So far, he was her dream guy. "And for the meal. I'm glad we didn't have to pay for my cold dinner, but I didn't mind paying for my half of your meal, really."

It wasn't like they were on a real date, and she understood that. When he'd changed seats, there'd been a flicker of hope that maybe she hadn't been reading too much into things and he might actually like her. That was dashed when Caroline realized he was only trying to get Ruthie to leave him alone. Not to mention that he'd made sure Ruthie knew they were there for planning and not a date.

He leaned his shoulder against her wall, facing her. "First, I invited you. Second, your food arrived cold, and third, it was my pleasure. I just wish Ruthie hadn't been so spiteful."

That woman had never liked Caroline. Not because of any one thing she'd ever done; Ruthie just didn't care for anyone who couldn't do something for her. A selfish streak ten miles wide ran down her back. She'd been pretty in high school and, of course, popular, which gave her a lot of clout.

Ruthie just never considered that high school would end. Once she was in the real world, treating people like they were dirt under her shoes didn't get her very far.

"She's always been like that."

"I know. That's why I never understood her popularity." He grunted a laugh. "When Zach started going with her, I was floored."

Caroline chewed her lip. "What I've learned since graduating high school is that it ends. Everything you have during those four years is all you have if you never plan for anything beyond."

Nodding, King said, "I agree, but I have to admit,

looking back, I could have made better decisions. I know I was self-absorbed."

"I think we all were."

The ensuing silence descended on them like a thick fog. Caroline had no idea what to say or talk about. So far, what she'd learned of King, she liked. He was sweet, chivalrous, and rugged. His hands were large and calloused and the sexiest thing she'd ever seen. A man who could work like that was worth gold in her opinion.

King cleared his throat, tipping his head in the direction of her old Cutlass. "So, do you know what's wrong with your car?"

"No, I guess I'm taking it to the shop on Monday. Maybe. I'll have to see if I can get a sub for the morning so I can." Hopefully, Pauline didn't have to be at the paper early and she could step in for Caroline.

"I'll take care of it."

Caroline's mouth dropped open. "What?"

King grinned. "I'll take care of your car. We have a new hand, my best friend from college, starting on the ranch tomorrow, and I have the whole weekend off. I could even take a look before I take it to the shop. I'm not a whiz, but I've worked on my share of cars. Maybe I can save you a little money."

She touched her hand to her chest. He was volunteering to look at her car on his day off. Talk about heart-melting. It was so kind of him to do such a thing. "You'd do that for me?"

"Sure. It's no big deal."

Huge deal was more like it. That car had given her grief since she'd purchased it. It was a money-eating machine. "That would be wonderful. I'd pay of course."

He shot her a heart-stopping grin. "Oh yeah? How about instead of paying me, you go on a date with me tomorrow night?"

Blinking, Caroline was sure she'd just hallucinated. King West couldn't have just asked her on a date. No way. No how. Didn't happen. "What?"

His smile widened as he chuckled. "A date. With me. Tomorrow."

Wow. Her thrumming heart sounded like a hummingbird trapped in her ear. She had to be hearing things. "You're asking me on a date?"

"Yes, Caroline Nell, I'm asking you on a date." He laughed. "If you have plans, I'll—"

"Yes." The word rushed out. "I'd really like that." More like love it.

"Then it's a date."

"A date," she whispered. "Okay."

King straightened and ran a thumb across her cheek. "You are so beautiful."

He'd said she was the prettiest girl he'd ever seen, but at the time, she thought he was just being nice because Ruthie was prowling instead of waitressing. Caroline had never considered he could be serious. Not that she was complaining. King West was everything she'd dreamed of and more.

"You think I'm beautiful?" Caroline asked.

"Darlin', that's just a fact." He stepped closer, holding her gaze.

Suddenly, her lips were on a heat-seeking mission with her heart's help. His lips were so, so very close, and he was giving her a smoldering look that would have any woman melting into a puddle.

"I'll see you tomorrow." She turned the doorknob, stepped back, and paused in the doorway.

The smile never left his face. "Yes, ma'am."

Before she could think it through, she rushed forward, lifted on her toes, and kissed his cheek. "Tomorrow."

Caroline quickly shut the door and leaned her back against it. Holy moly. King West was six feet of pure yumminess. If she were a gambling woman, she'd have bet the whole farm that he was going to kiss her.

Pushing off the door, she rolled her eyes. He was just flirting. She remembered what he was like in high school. That was King being King. Nice and friendly.

He didn't want to kiss plain ole her. The date was probably going to turn into a meeting about the festival. Her imagination was working in overdrive.

Time would prove her right. He'd pick her up, they'd share a meal, and then they'd talk festival. No reason to squeal or call Pauline. No reason at all.

CHAPTER 6

*A*djusting the collar on his overalls, King walked into the living room as Amos got home from working at the ranch. "Amos, hey."

Amos gave him a nod as he entered the house. "Hey. What a day. You weren't kidding when you said this job was a lot of work."

King chuckled. "You can't beat the setting, though. I love working there."

"True. And it's nice to be roommates again, even though I've barely seen you since I got here. I really appreciate it."

"No problem, man."

King had met Amos during his last two years of college. They were two of a handful of guys who weren't interested in partying every weekend. Instead, they'd crowd into a dorm room, have some snacks, and play video games.

Amos sat on the couch with a huff. "Why are you dressed in mechanic overalls...on a Sunday?"

"Remember that girl—woman—I was telling you about before you came?" King took a seat adjacent to Amos. "The one I've been seeing around town?"

His friend nodded. "Yeah."

"I spent last weekend working on her car and then spent this week taking her back and forth to work and festival-planning meetings." King smiled.

He'd come to hate that car over the last week. It had caused him to reschedule their date, and he'd still not figured out what was wrong with it. Finally, he'd called up a buddy and given him a rundown of what it was doing. King had a few things to try, and he was crossing his fingers that the car roared to life by the time he needed to leave to get ready for their date.

He hoped a kiss at the end came with it. After nearly kissing her last weekend, it had been almost more than he could handle not to kiss her and let the car rust into dust. He'd held off, though, getting to know her a little more.

"Nice. Does she know you're pretty good with a wrench? I think you single-handedly kept us all from walking everywhere." Amos sank lower in the couch and yawned.

King shrugged. "No, I didn't tell her. Good thing too, because that car is a mess. I don't know who worked on it last, but if I ever find them, I'm walloping them." Although, part of him wanted to shake their hand since they'd given him the chance to spend so much time with Caroline. "I'm going to try to get it going today, and then I'm taking her out tonight."

Amos exhaled slowly. "Sounds fun." He yawned. "I'm exhausted."

"Well, get some sleep." King grabbed his keys from the hook hanging next to the door. "I'll catch you when I get back to wash up before I take Caroline out."

"Later," Amos called as King headed out the door.

King's pulse slowly rose the closer he got to Caroline. When he reached her house, he parked the truck and strolled to the front door, hitting the doorbell just as the door swung open.

He took her in, and his heart jackhammered. Man, she was one sexy woman in her t-shirt and jeans. Her hair was pulled back into a ponytail, and it was long enough that the ends were lying on her shoulder. His gaze reached her bare toes, and she even had cute feet.

"Hi." Her voice only got sweeter each morning he

visited her. "It's pretty cold, so I made us some coffee today, if you'd like some."

Most mornings, Caroline would answer her door and have hot chocolate for him. She'd invited him in a few times, but they'd been brief as she was soon knee-deep in grading and talking to parents on the phone.

"I'd love some."

She waved him in, and he followed her through the living room and into the kitchen. The house smelled fantastic. "Are you cooking something?"

Shrugging she said, "Just some cookies."

"Cookies, huh?"

"You said you liked chocolate chip." She pulled two cups from a mug tree sitting on her counter. "I thought I'd make you some as a way to say thank you for working on my car and driving me back and forth to work this week."

Man, he liked her. His stomach was definitely the way to his heart. "You didn't have to do that. I don't mind working on your car, and I certainly don't mind taking you to work or picking you up."

As she poured the coffee, she shrugged one shoulder just slightly. "I know, but I wanted to bake some anyway, and since I knew you liked them, I figured it would keep me from eating too many."

"I'll definitely take a few. If they taste as good as

they smell, they'll be amazing." He tested the coffee and then took a sip. Spitting it back into the cup, he winced. "I'm sorry. It was hot." A hot mess. That was the worst coffee he'd ever consumed.

She took a sip of hers and grimaced. "Oh, this is terrible, and I followed the directions to a T." Her shoulders rounded. "I'm kinda terrible at making coffee."

Laughing, he nodded. "Yeah, that was pretty bad. Mind if I try?"

"Please do." She emptied her mug into the sink before taking his and doing the same. "I'm so sorry."

"That's all right. You'll make up for it with the cookies." He winked.

Oh, that sweet little blush. He could picture pressing light kisses on every inch it touched.

"I hope so." She picked up the end of her hair and twirled it around her finger. "I cheated a little. I asked my Grandma Jo to make some dough so I could cook it."

As he rinsed the coffee pot out, he asked, "When did you have time to do that?"

"Early this morning. My grandma gets up with the roosters, so I walked over there to get it." She lowered her gaze to the floor. "She's usually got some in her fridge to fix when anyone shows up."

39

King set the pot down. "You walked to get the dough? How far?"

"She's just a couple of blocks from here. It wasn't a big deal. My car has stranded me more than once." She lifted her head, and their gazes locked. "I just wanted you to know I appreciated your taking time out of your schedule to help me."

That sweet gesture was akin to downing an entire bottle of love potion. The longer he held her gaze, the harder it was to breathe.

Closing the gap between them, he brought his lips down to hers, holding them there a heartbeat, enjoying the softness of them.

Leaning back, wide eyes stared back at him as he brushed his fingers across her cheek. "Thank you for thinking of me."

Her lips parted. "Uh-huh."

"I'm a little torn at the moment."

"You are?" The words were breathy, and her chest rose and fell in rhythm to his.

Nodding, he said, "Yes, very, very torn." He trailed his fingers down along her jaw. "See, I'd like to kiss you a little more, but if I do, I'm not sure I'll want to stop."

"Oh." Her eyes closed as his fingers found her lips and traced them.

"I also said I'd fix your car, and I keep my word to beautiful, sweet women who bake me chocolate chip cookies." He pressed his lips against hers again. "So, you see my dilemma?"

Her head bobbed up and down as her eyes slowly opened. "I see."

Again, he traced her lips, knowing that if he didn't move away, he'd kiss her again and let the car rot. "Let me make us some coffee, and I'll get to work. Okay?"

"Uh-huh."

Taking an agonizing step back, he finished preparing the coffee. "I think I'll go get started on the car while it brews." It was as close to an ice bath as he was going to get, and he definitely needed to cool off.

"Sure."

Before temptation could grasp him harder, he strode out the house and to the car. Bracing his hands against the hood, he shook his head, trying to clear it. Wow. What a sensual, sexy woman.

Mercy, and he had a date with her tonight. Which meant the car needed to be fixed, especially knowing the prize might be the opportunity to kiss her again.

The date couldn't come quick enough, and he was more than looking forward to it.

CHAPTER 7

"Stop freaking out, Caroline," Pauline said between bites of an Oreo cookie from her spot in the middle of Caroline's bed. "Obviously, he likes you, or he wouldn't have kissed you or asked you out."

Having to reschedule the date last weekend was disappointing, but she'd appreciated that he was so willing to keep working on her car. They would think one thing was fixed, only to find that something else was messed up. Apparently, the previous owner had worked on it, and he hadn't done such a great job. They'd spent most of their Sunday outside dealing with it.

Holding a silver dress in front of her, Caroline examined how it looked in the mirror, turning one way and then the other. Maybe King did like her, but that didn't make her any less nervous. This was an official date. "I just…"

"Want it to be perfect."

Caroline faced her and nodded. "Yeah."

King West had kissed her. Twice. Not *kissed* her, but, wow, there had been Hulk-sized power in those two little kisses. He'd brushed her cheek and then traced her lips with those rough hands, and she was putty in them. She'd been so shocked that all her silly self could do was mumble agreements and bob her head like her neck was broken. The thick tension that morning would have needed a power saw to cut through it.

Then he'd worked on her car until he had no choice to go home to get ready. He was so cute in his overalls and grease smudges. Her car was not on his "favorites" list, but he'd promised to keep working on it until it was fixed. It was so sweet.

Of course, she'd bundled up and kept him company since she'd been unable to during the week since winter break was coming. There was a lot to do before they were out of school. It made the morning go quickly as she sat by his tools, handing them to him. He'd slide from under the car and flash her a smile, and her near-frozen self would warm like a portable heater was pointed directly at her.

Picking up another dress, Caroline's gaze roamed over her reflection. "He makes my heart skip beats. He's so sweet, Pauline."

"He sure is handsome. Wish he had a friend." She tossed an Oreo stripped of its cream filling back into the bag. At least it wasn't Caroline's Oreo bag. "Then we could double date."

Caroline faced her. "Actually, he said he did have a friend. His name is Amos, and he just started working at the ranch with King. That's why King had extra time off last weekend. Amos worked on a ranch in Arkansas before it went under. He was looking for a job."

Perking up, Pauline smiled. "Really?"

"King said he's a good guy. He's from New Mexico. They went to college together in Houston." Caroline picked up another dress, this time tossing it back down. Green was not her color. "King didn't say anything about a significant other."

"Wouldn't it be neat if we married men who were friends?" Pauline smiled.

Caroline nodded as she checked the time, and her heart raced. She was a mere hour from going on a date with King, and she could barely contain her excitement.

Spending time with him was magical, even if a little greasy at times. She'd learned they had so much in common. They shared common interests like reading, movies, and music. He loved kids and wanted a big family just like she did, at least four kids. They both liked simple things like snuggling together on a front porch swing or in front of the fireplace. It had been wonderful talking to him, and the more she found out, the more she liked him. He wasn't just a catch. King West was *the* catch. At least, for her he was.

"Wear the black one. You can't go wrong with a little black dress." Pauline propped herself on her elbow. "All guys like that."

Shaking her head, Caroline said, "Not King. His favorite color is blue." She picked up the light blue dress again, her mind made up. "This is the one."

Pauline nodded. "It's a good color on you, and if he likes blue, you'll knock his boots off."

Caroline sure hoped she did. She liked seeing him smile. Loved how he laughed, and the way her skin tingled when he touched her. It was easy to picture growing old with him, laughing and loving.

Stepping into the bathroom, she cracked the door as she pulled the dress over her head and zipped up the side. Opening the door, Caroline smoothed the skirt. "What do you think?"

"Oh, that's definitely the one. What are you doing with your hair?"

She faced the mirror. "I think curled."

Pauline nodded, scooted to the edge of the bed, and stood. "Okay, let's get it curled, then."

While her best friend styled her hair, she applied a smidge of makeup. Nothing too noticeable, just a tiny bit to bring out her eyes and a little lip gloss.

Once that was done, Caroline checked herself one more time just as the doorbell rang. Butterflies fluttered in her stomach. Would she stop feeling this nervous excitement? Hopefully, not.

She briskly walked out of her room with Pauline following and answered the door, her breath catching at the sight of him. He was to-die-for good-looking in his dress slacks and button-up shirt with a tie and suit coat. He'd even worn his nice cowboy boots. They'd talked about the ranch earlier in the day, and he'd mentioned buying a new pair.

"Hi," she said shyly.

His gaze raked from the top of her head to her toes. "Caroline Nell, you sure know how to make a man's heart skip a beat." He took a deep breath and let it out slowly. "My goodness, it should be a crime to look as beautiful as you do."

Her face warmed to the point where she wondered if it'd melt. Palming her cheek, she said, "Oh, stop."

Taking her hand, he pulled her to him. "Darlin', a woman like you should hear that every day because it's true." He pressed his lips to her forehead and smiled as he looked past her, sticking his hand out in a wave. "Hi, Pauline."

"Hey." She grinned, grabbing her coat from the hook next to the door and walked past Caroline and King. "I'll talk to you later." Her pace sped up, and she jogged down the walkway, across the street, and slipped inside her house.

King looked over his shoulder. "She lives across the street, huh?"

"We've known each other since we were kids. She's more like a sister than a best friend. I hope if, or when, I have kids, our children will feel about each other the way we do. I couldn't imagine life without her. We've always done things together. We—" She stopped short. "I'm rambling."

A smile lifted the corners of his lips. "Adorably so." He bent and kissed her nose before taking her coat from the hook next to the door and helping her into it.

"But I think that about all of you. You ready for dinner?"

Nodding, she grinned as her cheeks warmed. This man. Oh, this man made every inch of her gelatin. If things kept going this way, she'd be head over heels for him in no time. Not that she had all that far to go in the first place.

Inwardly, she scolded herself for moving entirely too fast. They'd spent time together the past week, but this was their first official date. Maybe he wasn't thinking anything beyond this. She had enough self-respect not to throw herself at someone, even if he was fantastic and his name made her tongue tingle. Slow. She needed to slow down and just take things as they came, no matter what her heart had to say about the situation.

CHAPTER 8

*G*lancing at Caroline, King inhaled and exhaled slowly. She smelled good, she looked good, and there wasn't a flaw in anything she had on, from her hair to the tips of her silver heels. If there ever was an angel who fell to earth, it was her.

Her knee-length soft blue dress made her a vision, and, man, did the woman have shapely legs. The little peacoat she'd slipped on over it made her look every bit the runway model. To top it off, she'd left her hair down, and it hung in curls to her shoulders. Mercy, his fingers physically ached to touch it. He could picture the dark waterfall slipping through his fingers like silk.

"We're going here?" Caroline asked as King parked

the truck and cut the engine. "It's the nicest restaurant in Amarillo."

"That's what I've heard. I figured we'd try it out." He smiled, getting out of the truck and walking around the front.

As he opened the door, she pushed a piece of her hair back and said, "Thank you for taking me to dinner. It's been a while since I've been...on a date." The last two words were just above a whisper.

What sort of men laid eyes on a woman like her and walked on by? Granted, in his youth, he'd been oblivious, but now, he was smart enough to acknowledge a treasure when he saw it. He took her hand in his, helping her out of the truck.

"Blind men, I say, and good for me. I'll have the prettiest, sexiest woman on my arm tonight." He flattened his palm on the small of her back, pulling her flush against him. "I'm am one lucky fella."

"Oh." She covered her cheek with her free hand. "I blush every time you say something like that."

Cupping her cheek, he lifted her gaze to his. "My grandad, Henry, always said a man's job was to make a woman blush. I don't think there was a day that went by that my grandmamma didn't blush from something he said or the way he kissed her. He said that he'd promised himself their honeymoon would never end." He brushed his thumb across her lips. "And it didn't."

Her breath quickened as her lips parted.

The temptation to kiss her had never been stronger, but he'd made himself a promise that he'd take her to dinner and then kiss her. He didn't want a growling stomach to interrupt him.

"He must have loved her a lot. I bet she loved him too."

Nodding, King leaned closer, holding her gaze. "They loved each other. They taught me I didn't need music to dance with the person I cared about. All I needed was a heart beating in rhythm with mine. Do you like to dance?"

Caroline whispered, "I do."

He liked those words coming from her lips. *Settle down, boy,* his head said, while his heart yelled, *Sold.* It was their first date, after all. He didn't want to scare her off, but it was hard to hold himself back when his gut was telling him she was the one.

One thing he was sure of, his search was over. If it took a year or five, Caroline Nell was it for him.

Based on the hitch in her breath and the way she stared at him, he got the impression she felt the same way, but until he was sure, he'd go slow and steady. She was worth the wait.

CHAPTER 9

The evening spent with King couldn't have been better even in a dream. When it came to spending time with him, she would have been happy no matter what they were doing. Watching grass grow would be fantastic if he was holding her.

The truck rattled as it went over rough dirt, shaking her from her thoughts. "Where are we?"

"I thought we'd enjoy the new moon and meteor shower. We're just a few miles past town. Should be bright and clear out here."

She'd been so lost in how wonderful her evening was that she had no idea they'd driven right through town. "Oh."

He smiled. "Don't worry. I won't let you freeze." He winked.

Oh, when he did that, she couldn't help but see them dancing to no music. Just his smile, the sound of his heartbeat, and her. It was such a sweet story, and the way he'd seemed to be talking to her had liquified her insides.

When the truck was parked, he kept the headlights on, which was a good idea with as pitch-black dark as it was. He unbuckled his seatbelt, got out, and came around to her side, opening her door. She loved that he opened doors for her.

Taking her hand, he helped her out and never loosened his hold on her hand as they walked to the back of his pickup.

He dropped the tailgate and pulled a folded pile of blankets closer, spreading them out so they wouldn't be sitting directly on hard metal. "I'm sorry they're cold, but with a single cab pickup, the best place I could find was back here."

As warm as she was, a cool blanket didn't sound too bad. "That's okay. I don't think I've ever watched a meteor shower in the dark like this." She looked at the distance between the tailgate and the ground. In jeans, it would be no problem to get on it, but in a dress and heels? "I don't think I can get up there without losing my dignity."

Taking her by the waist, he gently set her on the

tailgate. "That okay?"

"Uh-huh." That seemed to be her go-to anytime he touched her, but she couldn't help it when it seemed he snipped the wires to her brain each time. "I mean, thank you."

"Let me get the headlights off, and then we'll watch for the shower." He left her, and she twisted to watch him walk back to the cab. Once the lights were out, he shut his driver door and used the pickup as a guide to make his way back.

She squeaked when the truck moved with his weight as he sat. "Sorry."

"That's all right. Out at the ranch, I get to enjoy this kind of dark when there's a new moon, but for most, this is a little scary."

"Yeah," she said, hearing more critters make noise the longer the lights were out. She didn't realize there'd be so many in winter. She shivered as a small icy breeze hit her face. "It's a little cold out here with no buildings to block the wind."

King put his arm around her and pulled her close. "Here." He grabbed a blanket and spread it over them. "Better?"

Caroline didn't need a blanket with him holding her. Snuggling closer, she leaned her head against his chest. "It's great."

This was the kind of together she could easily get used to. Him holding her under a blanket of stars and not another soul in sight. He seemed as content as she was when minute after minute ticked by with neither of them breaking the silence that descended.

It made her think about her parents before they moved to Florida, leaving her their house. They'd dated a long time before they got married, and her mom was more about practical things than wishes and dreams.

Before she knew what her lips were doing, Carolina asked, "Don't read anything into this, but do you believe in love at first sight? My mom always told me it was a fairy tale, but I sometimes wonder if it's true."

The longer he was silent, the more worried she became. She wasn't telling him she loved him or even wondering if he could ever see himself loving her. It was just a silly question that didn't even apply to them since they'd seen each other many times while they were in school together.

Just when she thought he'd never answer, he cleared his throat. "I think sometimes it is. Maybe, on occasion, someone will think they're in love when it's just loneliness speaking."

Nodding, she put her index finger to her mouth

and nibbled on it. "I think you're right."

"Have you ever had that happen?" His breath hit her cheek, and his voice was low.

"No..." Not yet. She was sure questioning it now, though. King had given her all sorts of whimsical notions. "Not yet. Have you?"

There was a small pause. "I'm reserving judgment for the moment." There was a hint of playfulness in his voice.

It made her heart take off like a rocket. *Reserving judgment.* That sounded about right. She'd debated it many times, but King was giving her plenty to consider.

At one point, she'd been certain that her mom was right. There was no such thing as love at first sight because it took work to build a friendship strong enough to carry a marriage. Sitting with King in the dark, waiting for a meteor shower, was bringing a fairy tale to life for her.

Once the shower began, they took turns pointing different ones out. It was funny to her that something so simple could be so exciting. It was a beautiful show, too. Next time she heard about one coming, she'd find a way to let her students experience it.

By the time they drove back to Caprock Canyon, Caroline was working on breaking the world record for yawning. She was exhausted, but she'd have sat on that tailgate all night long if it meant staying in King's arms.

As they reached her door, Caroline faced him. "I had such a wonderful time tonight. Thank you for... well, everything."

King pulled her closer. "The pleasure was all mine."

"The meteor shower was beautiful."

"It was, but you beat it by a mile, and I can't hold it in my arms, which means you definitely win in my book." He brought his lips down to hers, and for the second time that night, she saw stars.

Dropping her purse on the porch, she circled her arms around his neck. The rush of blood in her ears drowned out the pounding of her heart.

A deep moan came from his throat as he coaxed her lips to part, and warmth spread from her core, sending her blood rushing even faster. The kiss grew demanding as he threaded his fingers through her hair and cupped the back of her head.

"So soft," he murmured against her lips before deepening the kiss once again.

Her lips were sore by the time he broke the kiss, brushing his lips along her cheeks, down her neck, and back to her lips.

Touching his forehead to hers, he gulped air.

"Caroline."

"Yes," she said, her breath shaky.

"I'd stand here and kiss you all night, but you have school tomorrow."

"It's a half-day." She ran the tip of her nose along his jawline. "I only have to be half-awake."

Laughter rumbled from him. "Is that so?"

"Uh-huh."

The words were barely out before he crushed his lips to hers in a kiss that was more toe-curling than the last. Pressing his hand flat against her back, he pressed her so hard against his body that she could feel the muscles tense as his hold tightened. She'd never kissed or been kissed like this. It felt like he was trying to drink her in, and he couldn't get enough. She certainly couldn't.

By the time they broke the kiss, Caroline's head was swimming and her lungs were burning. Did love at first sight really happen? Maybe. Did love at first kiss happen? Most definitely. She'd fallen for King West, and there wasn't any chance of recovery. If he wanted her even half as much as she wanted him, they'd love a lifetime and beyond.

The thought startled her, but she couldn't deny how she felt. She belonged to him, head, heart, and soul.

*a*s King stood in the high school gym, it took work to keep his mind on the festival when all he could think about was Caroline. He was in charge of finishing up decorations and getting tables to the right spots while Caroline was getting the supplies needed to have the hot chocolate cook-off.

After their kiss Sunday night, the pep in his step was nonstop. That kiss had boiled his blood and given him a fever only she could cure. It had taken every ounce of his willpower to leave her that night, but he'd done it...and taken a long, very cold shower.

The past week since, it had become a nightly routine. Did he believe in love at first sight? He'd told her he was reserving judgment. Not anymore. Since he'd the moment he'd laid eyes on her after returning home, she was all he saw. He was head over heels for her and loved her with every inch of his heart.

Waking up to snow on the ground that morning had given him the sign he'd needed. The festival the next evening was going to be one that would either carry him to heaven or break his heart.

A tap on the shoulder had him wheeling around, expecting Caroline, only to find Ruthie Dunn in front of him. The smile on his face vanished. "Hey, Ruthie."

"Hey," she said and shifted on her feet. "I wanted to tell you I was sorry for that night at the diner. It was rude of me. I shouldn't have been like that. I guess my divorce hit me a lot harder than I'm willing to admit, even now."

King knew Ruthie had been a little manipulative in high school, which meant he didn't trust her now either. Still, if she was making amends, he'd been taught to give people the chance to be better. "I appreciate that. I hope you'll let Caroline know that too."

"Thank you. I promise I'll tell her." She threw her arms around his neck and kissed him.

A loud gasp startled him as he pulled free of Ruthie, and he saw Caroline bolting out of the gym.

"Stay," he yelled at Ruthie as he took off for Caroline. "I'll be back."

He reached the door of the gym and, looking both ways, spotted Caroline walking in the direction of her house. Taking off at a run, he quickly caught up with her. "Caroline."

"It's okay, King."

He took her by the arm and spun her to face him. Tears streaked down her cheeks, and his heart broke. "I know what you thought you saw, but I can assure you it wasn't at all like you think."

"I know. That's why I was walking away. I had a kneejerk reaction, and I wanted a chance to think it through." She furiously wiped away tears. "I trust you. I do."

Pulling her flush against him, he held her tight. "I appreciate that."

After holding her a moment, he said, "Sweetheart, there's isn't a woman in this town that I want more than you. I'm sorry that hateful thing hurt you." He kissed the top of her head. "Now, come with me."

King released her and laced his fingers in hers as they walked back to the gym where Ruthie stood, a smile plastered on her face until her gaze hit Caroline.

Ruthie crossed her arms over her chest. "Really? Her?"

King narrowed his eyes. "Yes, absolutely her. Every day, all day, her. I pick her. She's my girl, and if you—"

Caroline stuck her chin out. "And if you ever put your lips on him again, I'll slug you so hard you'll see the back of your head. I love him, and he's mine."

Rolling her eyes, Ruthie dropped her arms. "Whatever. You'll probably last as long as me and Zack." She stormed out of the gym.

King turned to Caroline, his heart hitting a pace he was sure it had never reached before. "You love me, huh?"

She lowered her gaze, rolling her lips in. "It kinda just flew out."

"Darlin', I like that kind of flying." He wrapped his arms around her. "I love you too, Caroline."

Leaning back, a smile lifted her lips. "You do?"

Nodding, he said, "With all my heart." He paused. "Would you be my date for the festival?"

Her arms circled his chest. "I'd love to."

"Then it's a date," he said, leaning back. "But I think that means we need to get in gear since it's tomorrow."

A smile lit up her face, and her eyes sparkled. "Okay. I'm almost done getting the kids in their places, and they're rehearsing now."

"All right. Let get this done, then. I think the festival is going to be all sorts of fun this year." He winked.

Caroline caught her bottom lip in her teeth. "Me too."

King kissed her before letting her go back to work. Oh yeah, tomorrow night was going to be amazing.

CHAPTER 11

*R*ushing through the path carved out of the snow, Caroline held a container of cocoa in one hand and marshmallows in the other. Mrs. Jeter, one of the competitors in the hot chocolate cook-off, had dropped her can, and it had gone everywhere. They had thirty minutes to get their cocoa ready to be judged, and it wasn't even her fault. One of the kids from the choir was playing and had run smack into her.

"Oh, thank you, Caroline," Mrs. Jeter said as she took the ingredients. "I'm sorry."

"It's okay." Caroline shrugged. "Good luck."

She reached the area where the snowman contest had just ended and smiled as the winners were announced. A moment later, an arm curled around her waist, and King's lips were against her ear.

"Hey, sweetheart. You mind taking a sleigh ride with me?"

A tiny giggle trickled out as his breath tickled her. "Sure."

Oh, she loved him. She loved him with all her heart and then some. It had slipped out the day before, and for a second, she'd wondered if she'd ruined things. When he returned those three little words, she'd nearly passed out. She'd wanted desperately to hear them because she knew that's how she felt.

Whatever stunt Ruthie thought she was pulling was over before it had begun. Confronting her had given Caroline a new confidence she didn't know she possessed. No one was going to come between her and King. She loved him, and he loved her.

They reached the sleigh, and King shook the driver's hand. "Amos, this is Caroline Nell. Amos Fredericks, this is Caroline."

"It's nice to finally meet you," Amos said, shaking her hand.

"You too." Caroline smiled.

Yep, Amos and Pauline would need to meet. If Caroline knew her best friend, and she did, Amos was Pauline's kind of man. Shorter than King by just an inch or two, tanned skin and handsome, and nice enough to drive a sleigh after working at a ranch all day.

"Thank you for doing this for the school," she added. "I really appreciate it."

"Oh, no problem." He grinned at King. "Did he tell you he sold that new pickup he had a couple of weeks ago to help pay for some of it?"

King grumbled loudly. "I told you not to tell her that."

Caroline faced King. "You did?"

His neck turned red, and it rose to his face. "I just thought my kids would one day be going to school and they'd need a decent place to play. It was an investment in the future."

Lifting up, Caroline kissed him. It was the sweetest, most selfless thing to do. A Texan and his truck were hard to part. That he'd done something like that meant he was one in a million. "I love your heart."

A smile lifted his lips, reaching his eyes. "I love your heart." He dropped to one knee.

Caroline's hands flew to her face. "Oh."

"I was going to wait until we were on the sleigh, but I think this is the perfect moment." He pulled a ring from the pocket inside his coat. "This ring belonged to my grandma. My grandad gave it to me before he died and told me that I'd know the woman it belonged to when I saw her."

People gathered in a circle around them, murmuring.

King continued, "You're it for me. Love at first sight was a notion that was more fairy tale than real until I met you." He paused. "Caroline Nell, will you marry me? I'd be living a half-life with anyone but you."

Tears ran down her cheeks as she nodded. "I will. I will marry you."

He rose to his feet and slipped the ring on her finger. "I love you, Caroline. With all of me, forever and ever. You're the only dance partner I'll ever want."

She threw her arms around his neck and kissed him. Forever. It would never get old. She'd never let it. She'd spend her life loving him.

EPILOGUE

A few years later...

BREATHING HEAVY, King smiled as the sound of a baby's cry filled the room. Tears pooled in Caroline's eyes as he cut the cord. After quickly checking him over, the nurse handed the baby boy to Caroline.

There had never been a more beautiful sight. The love of his life holding his brand-new little boy. King wiped at his eyes. There was joy in marrying Caroline, excitement for their future, but watching his son come into the world was an experience he'd not been prepared for. He'd known he'd love the baby, but he'd not expected the grip their seven-pound-ten-ounce bundle would have on King's heart.

"Oh, King, he's beautiful," Caroline whispered.

Perfect was more like it. Ten fingers, ten toes, and a head full of dark hair. "Yes, my love, he's as perfect a baby as has ever been in this room." King ran his hand over the baby's head. "Does he look like a Bear to you?"

Caroline slipped her finger into the baby's hand, and his fingers curled around as he began to nurse. "I think so." She looked up at him with tired eyes and a faint smile. "I think he's our Bear."

"Then Bear it is."

She lowered her gaze to the baby again. "Bear," she said and kissed his cheek. "You are so wanted and loved."

King took Bear's toes in his hand. "More than I thought possible."

Their story had begun at *I do*, and now a new life would add to the ever-growing tale. King had no idea his life could be so rich. Some would call him lucky, but his grandad had another word: blessed. He'd been blessed with a life he could have only dreamed of. One that he was grateful for.

❄

Thanks for reading Her Christmas Crush! I hope you enjoyed King and Caroline's love story. If you'd like to continue the series, you can head over to Amazon. Just click here.

You can find me on Facebook, Twitter, YouTube, and Instagram. I also have a website www. breelivingston.com. You can even email me @breelivingston@breelivingston.com. I'd love to hear from you. Thanks again for reading my story.

ABOUT THE AUTHOR

Bree Livingston lives in the West Texas Panhandle with her husband, children, and cats. She'd have a dog, but they took a vote and the cats won. Not in numbers, but attitude. They wouldn't even debate. They just leveled their little beady eyes at her and that was all it took for her to nix getting a dog. Her hobbies include...nothing because she writes all the time.

She loves carbs, but the love ends there. No, that's not true. The love usually winds up on her hips which is why she loves writing romance. The love in the pages of her books are sweet and clean, and they definitely don't add pounds when you step on the scale. Unless of course, you're actually holding a Kindle while you're weighing. Put the Kindle down and try again. Also, the cookie because that could be the problem too. She knows from experience.

Join her mailing list to be the first to find out publishing news, contests, and more by going to her website at https://www.breelivingston.com.

facebook.com/BreeLivingstonWrites
instagram.com/breelivwrites
bookbub.com/authors/bree-livingston
amazon.com/author/breelivingston
youtube.com/BreeLivingstonAuthor
twitter.com/breelivwrites

Made in the USA
Monee, IL
14 February 2025

12250203R00049